Blueberry Girl

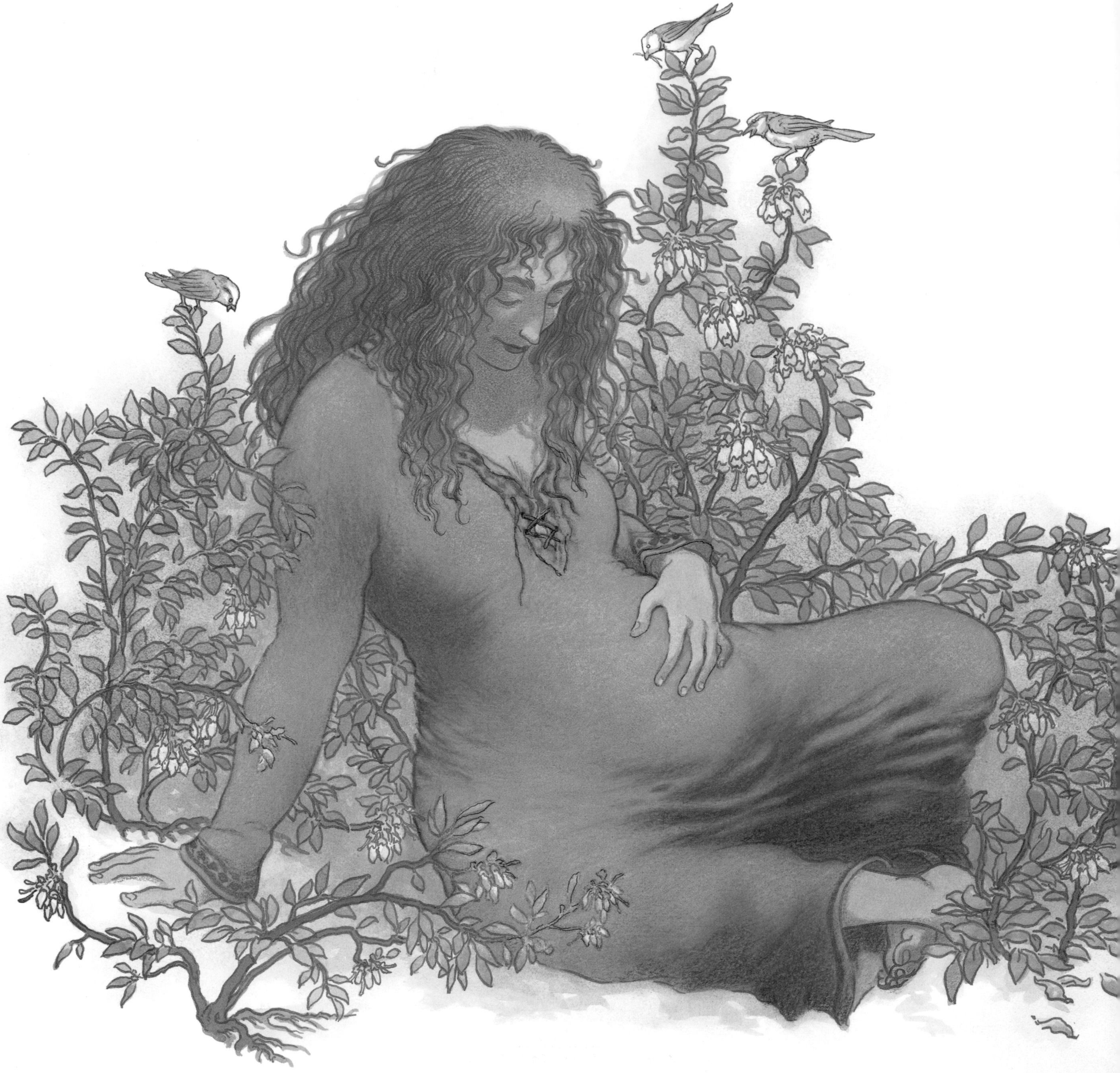

Blueberry Girl

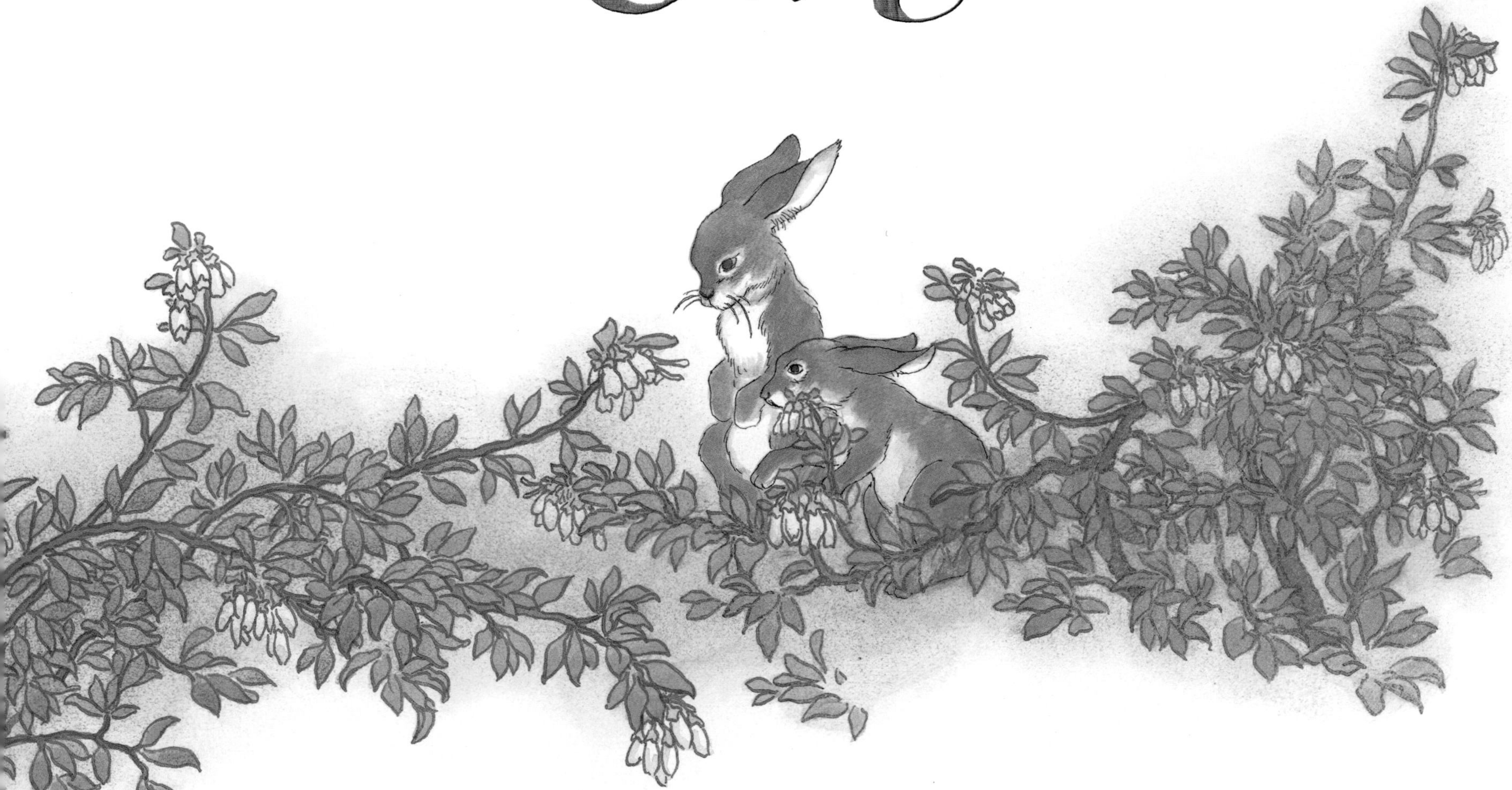

written by Neil Gaiman
illustrated by Charles Vess

HARPER
An Imprint of HarperCollinsPublishers

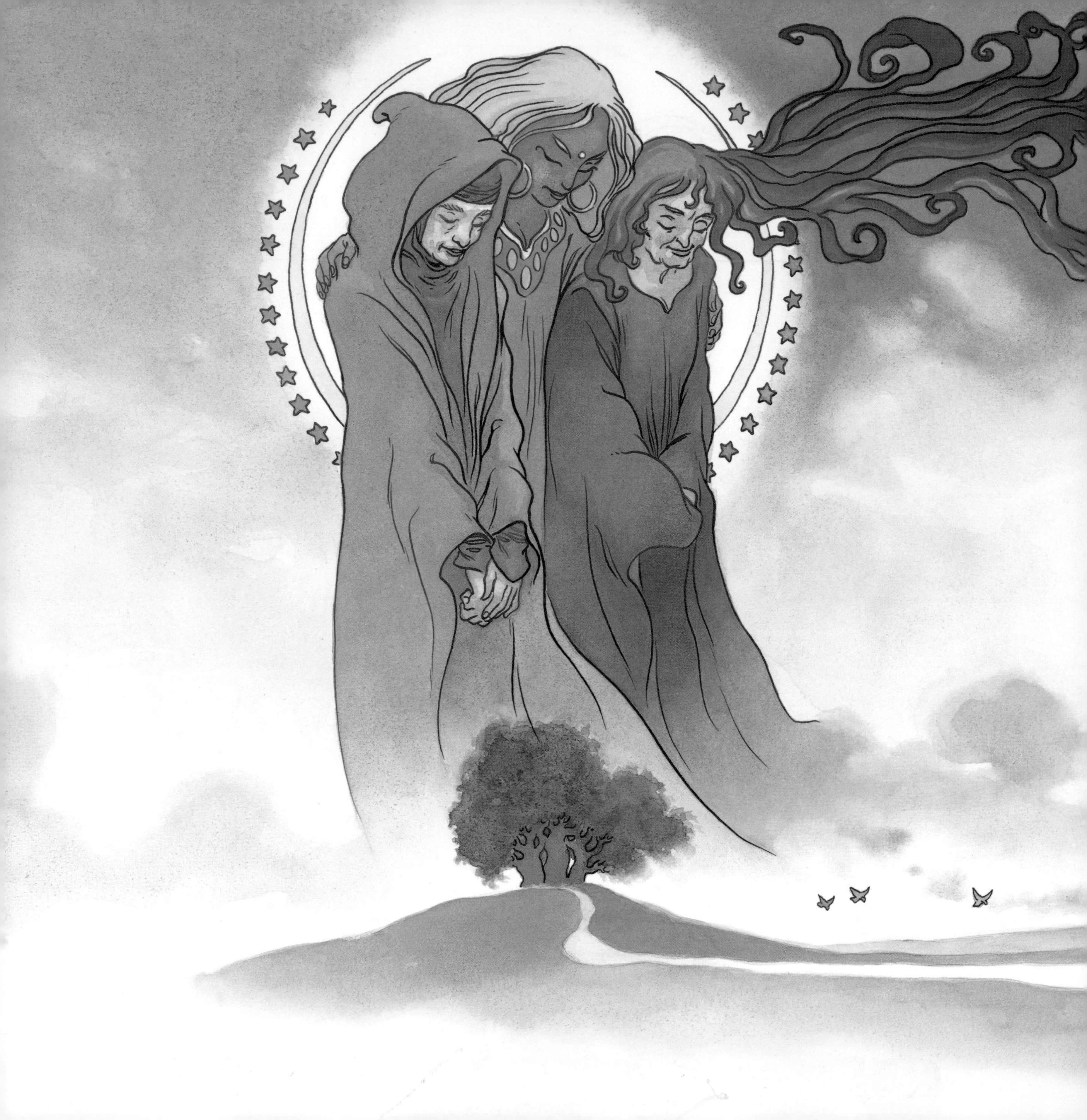

Ladies
of
light
and
ladies
of
darkness
and
ladies
of
never-
you-
mind,

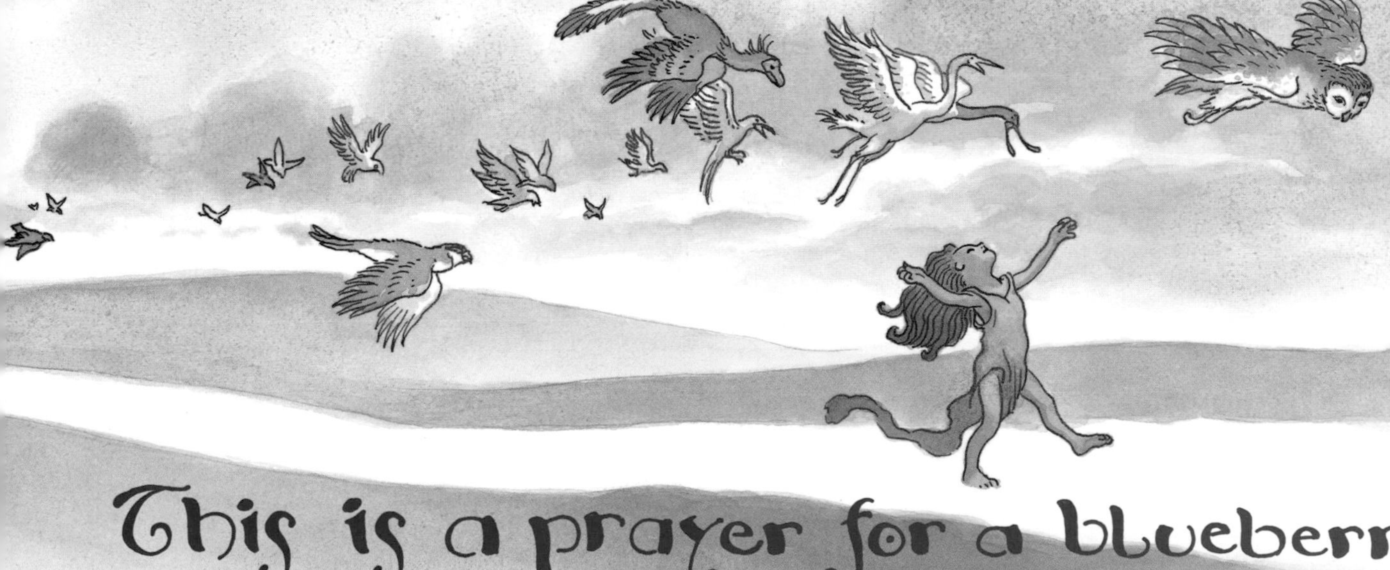

This is a prayer for a blueberry girl.

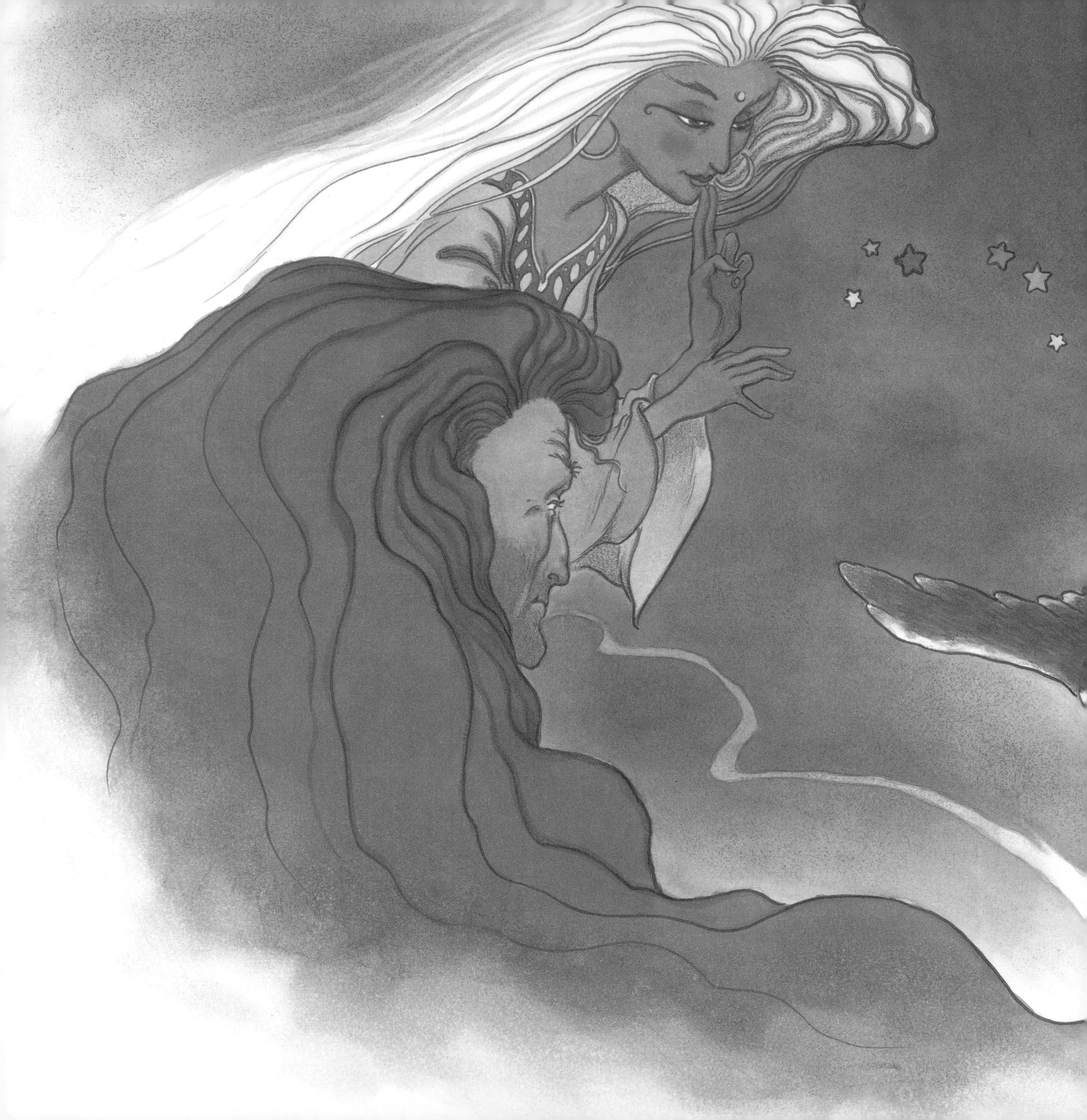

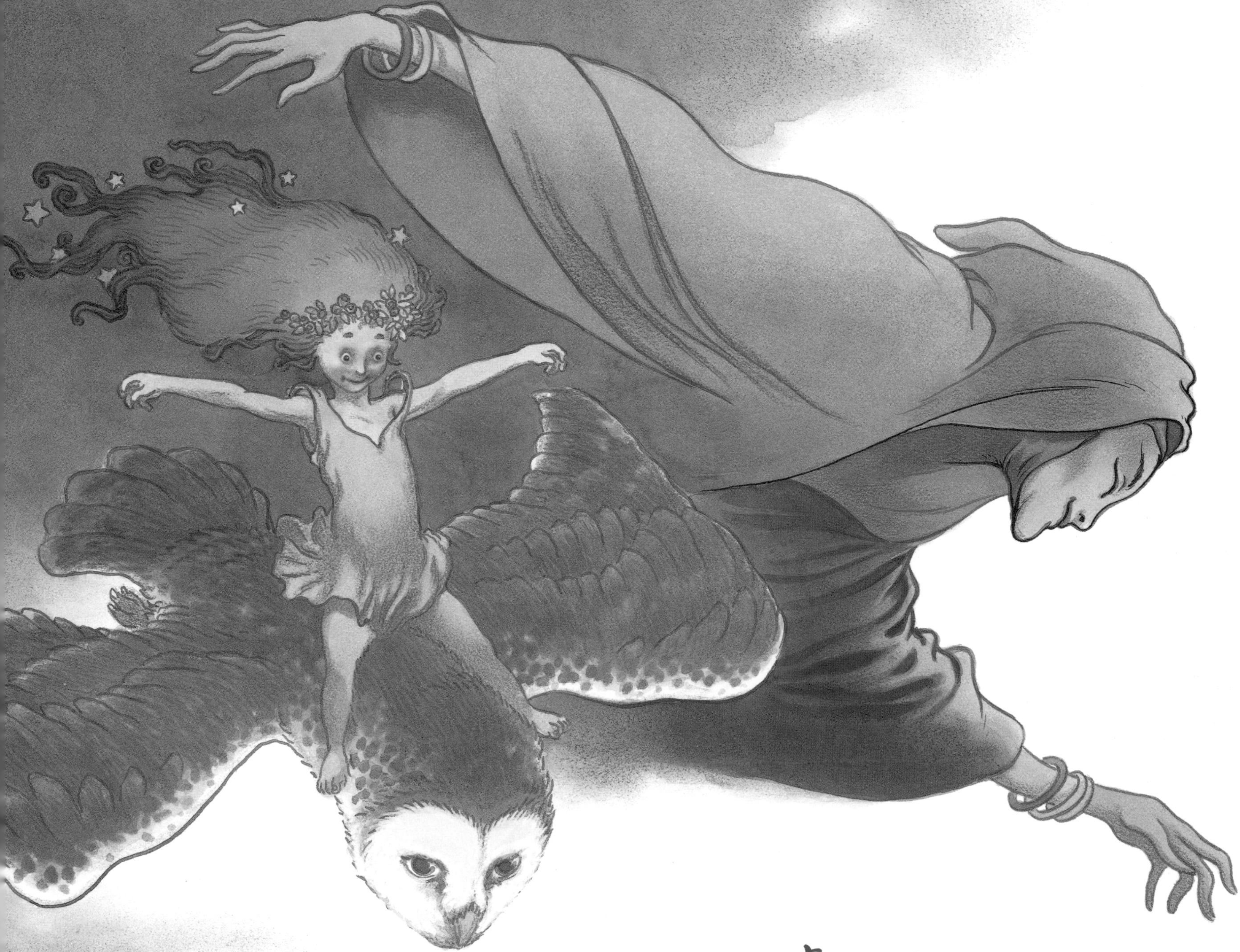

First, may
you
ladies
be kind.

Keep
her
from
spindles
and
sleeps
at
sixteen,

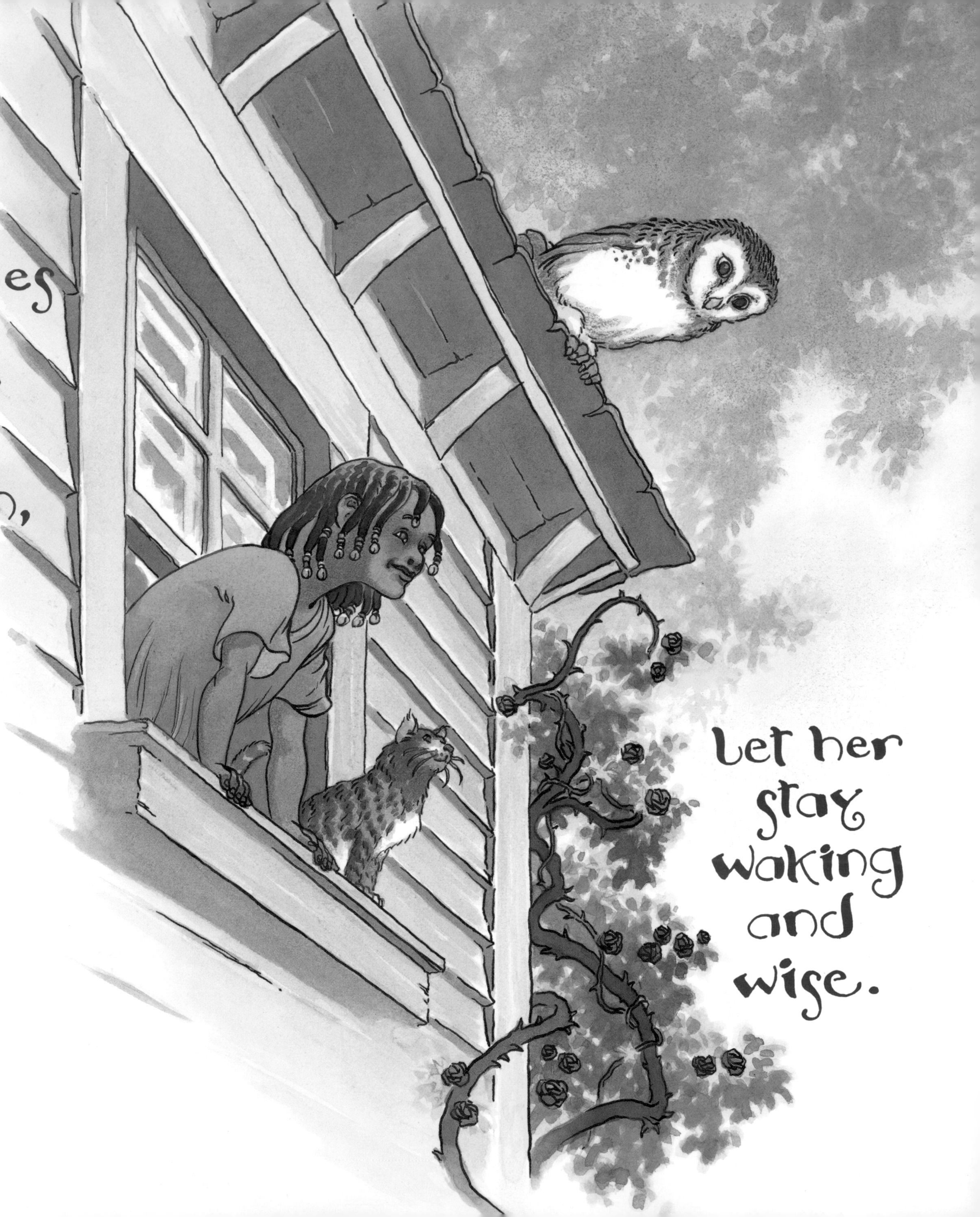

Let her
stay
waking
and
wise.

Nightmares at three or bad husbands at thirty,

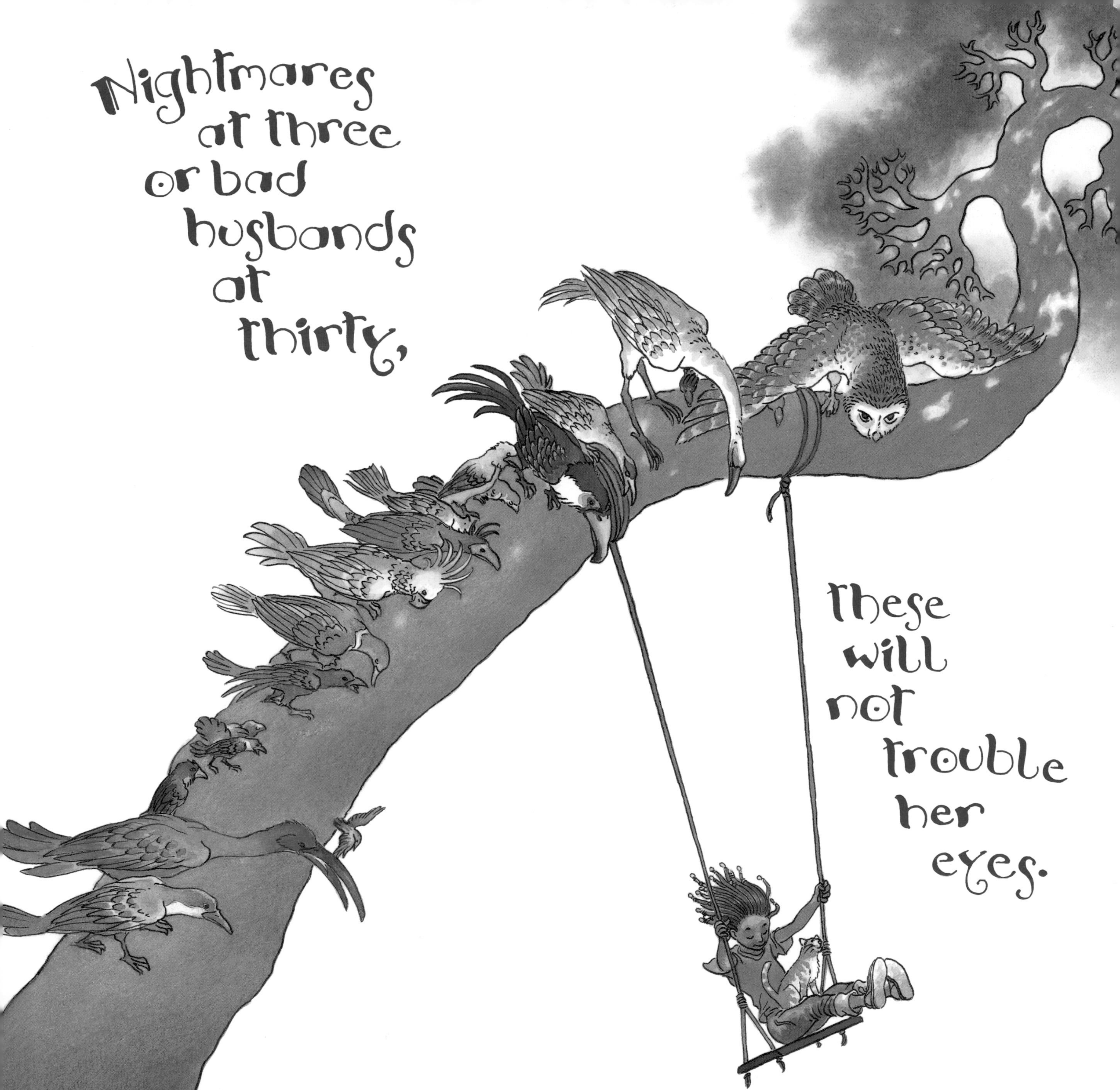

These will not trouble her eyes.

Dull days at forty,
false friends at fifteen—
let her have
brave days
and
truth,

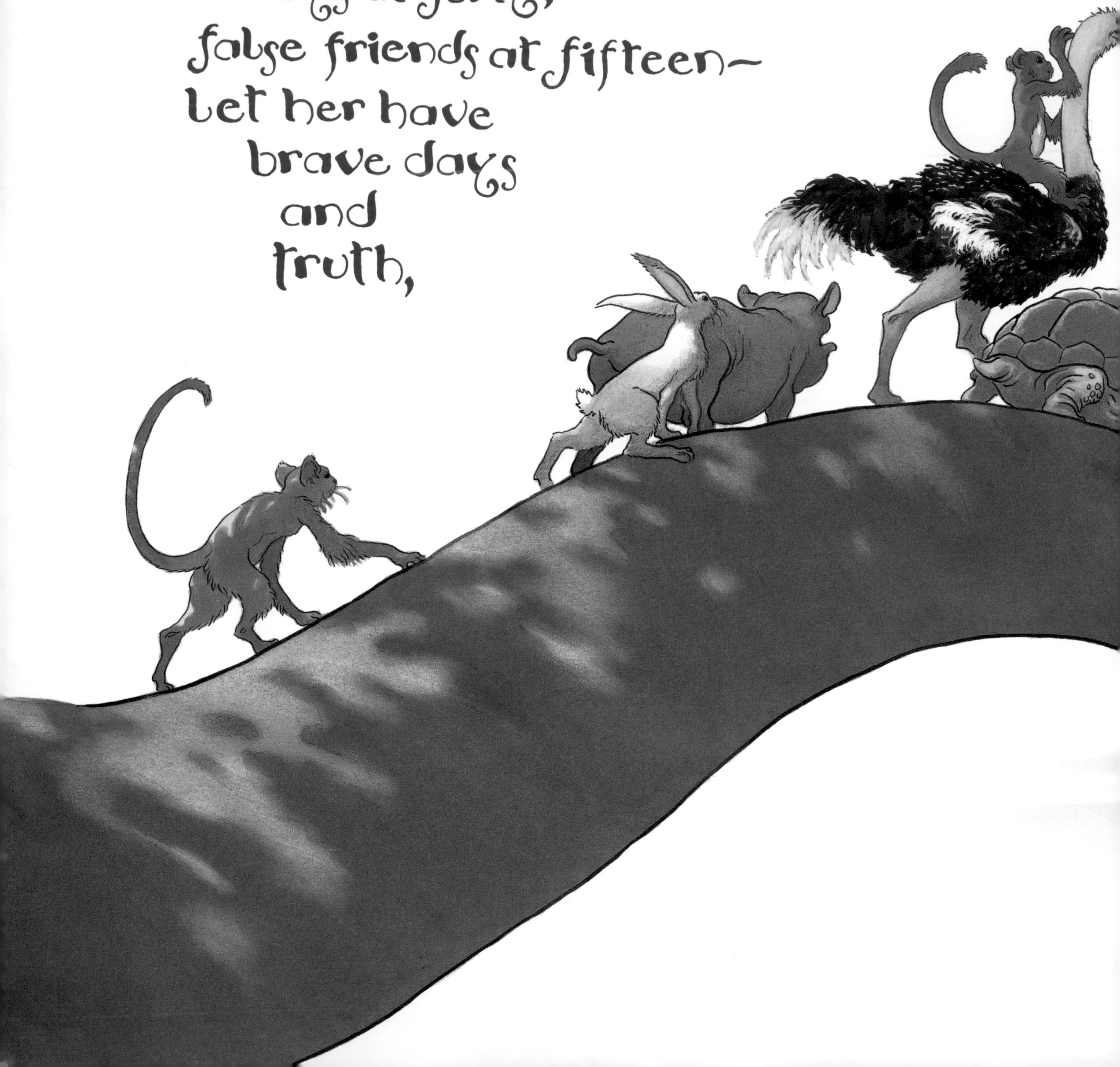

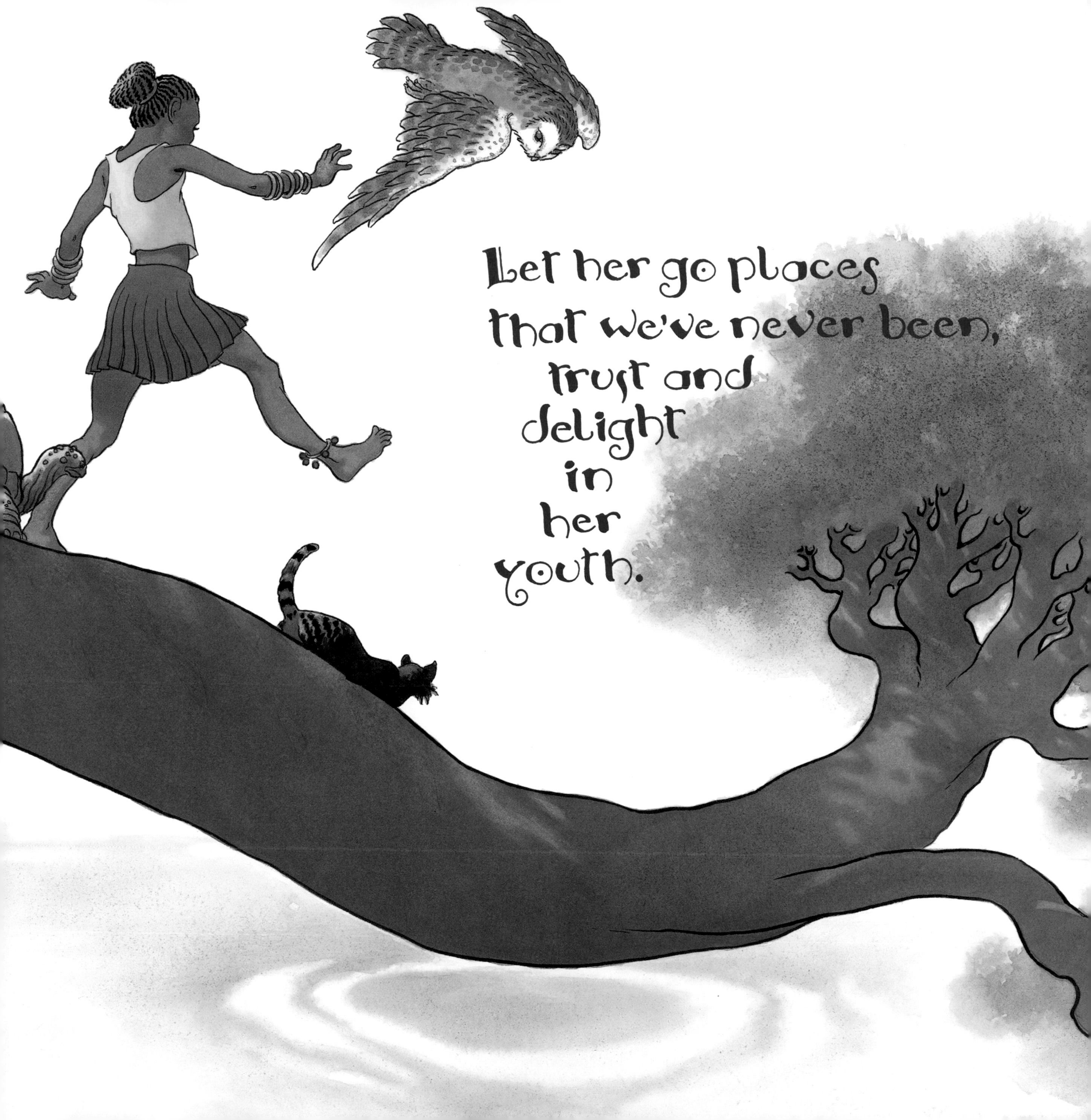

Let her go places
that we've never been,
trust and
delight
in
her
youth.

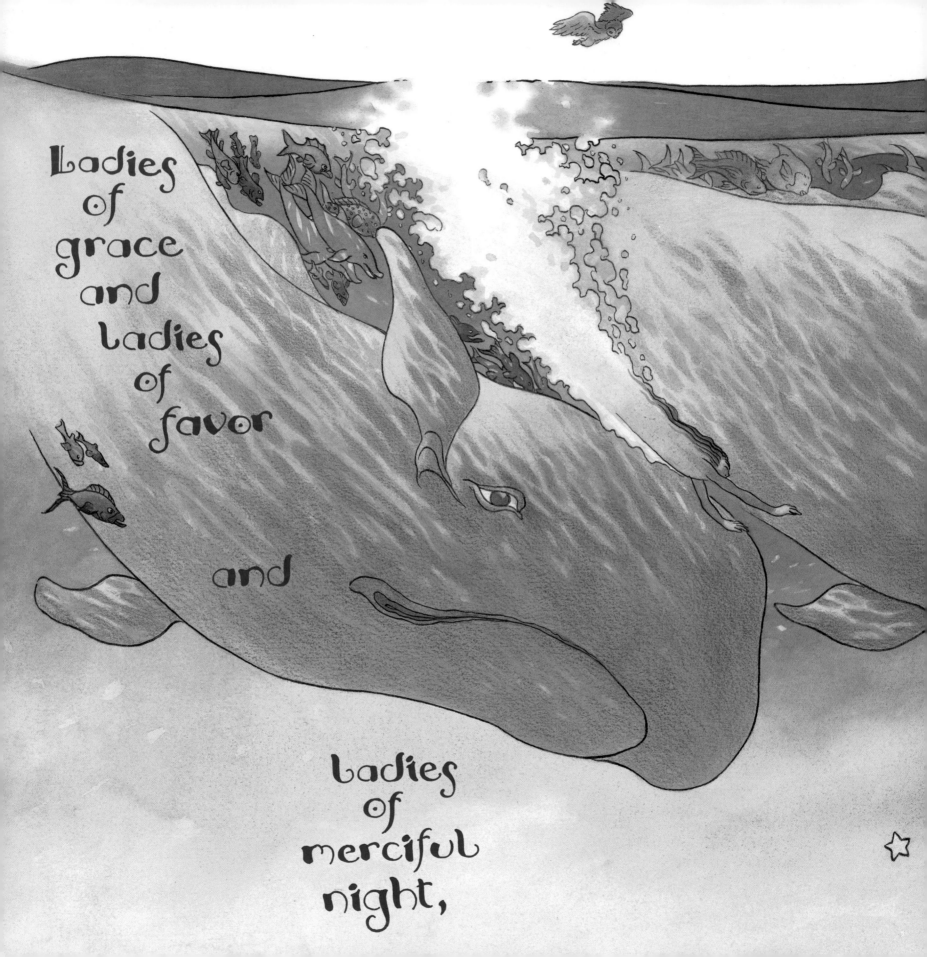

Ladies
of
grace
and
ladies
of
favor

and

Ladies
of
merciful
night,

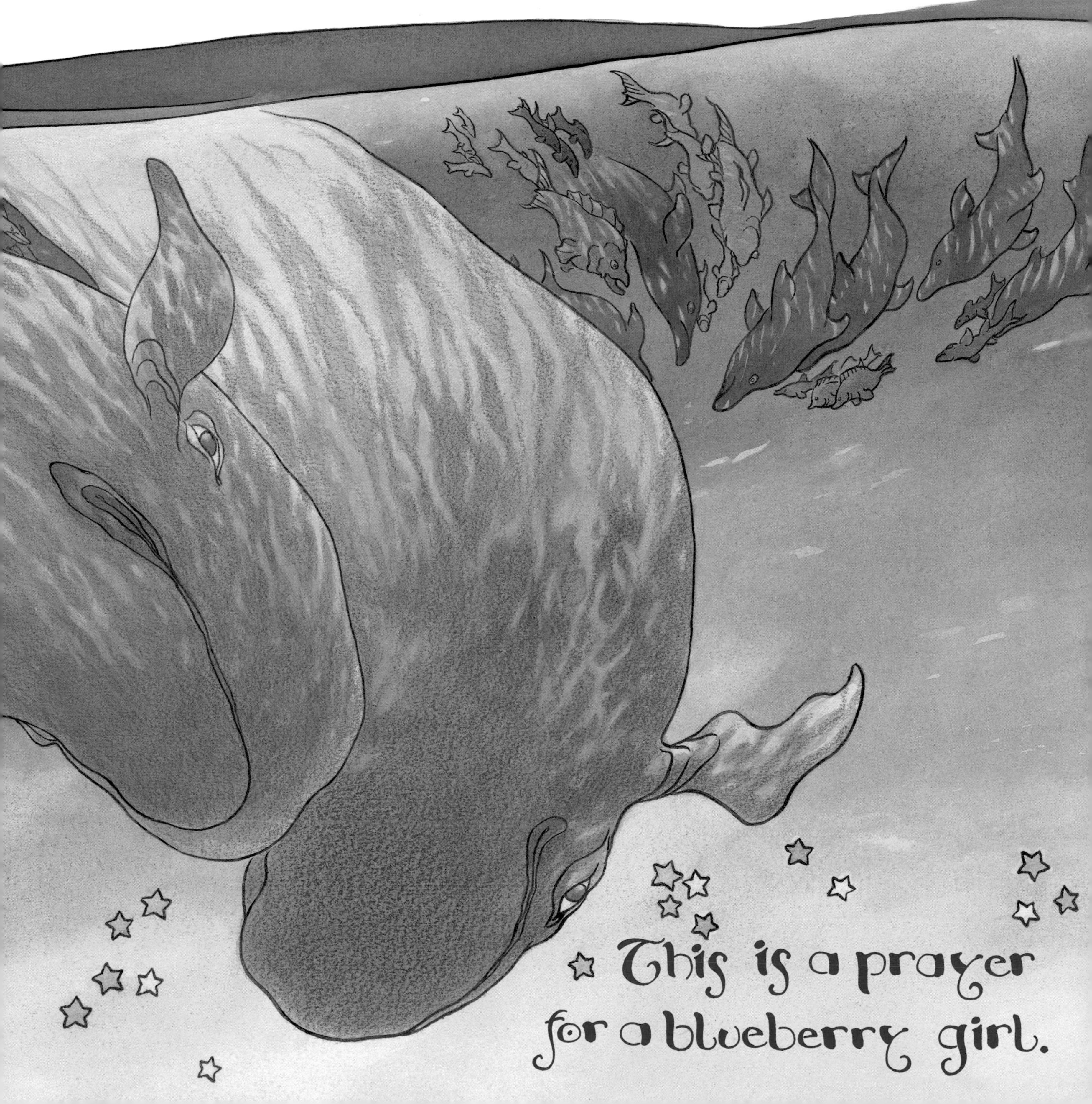

This is a prayer
for a blueberry girl.

Grant
her your
clearness
of
sight.

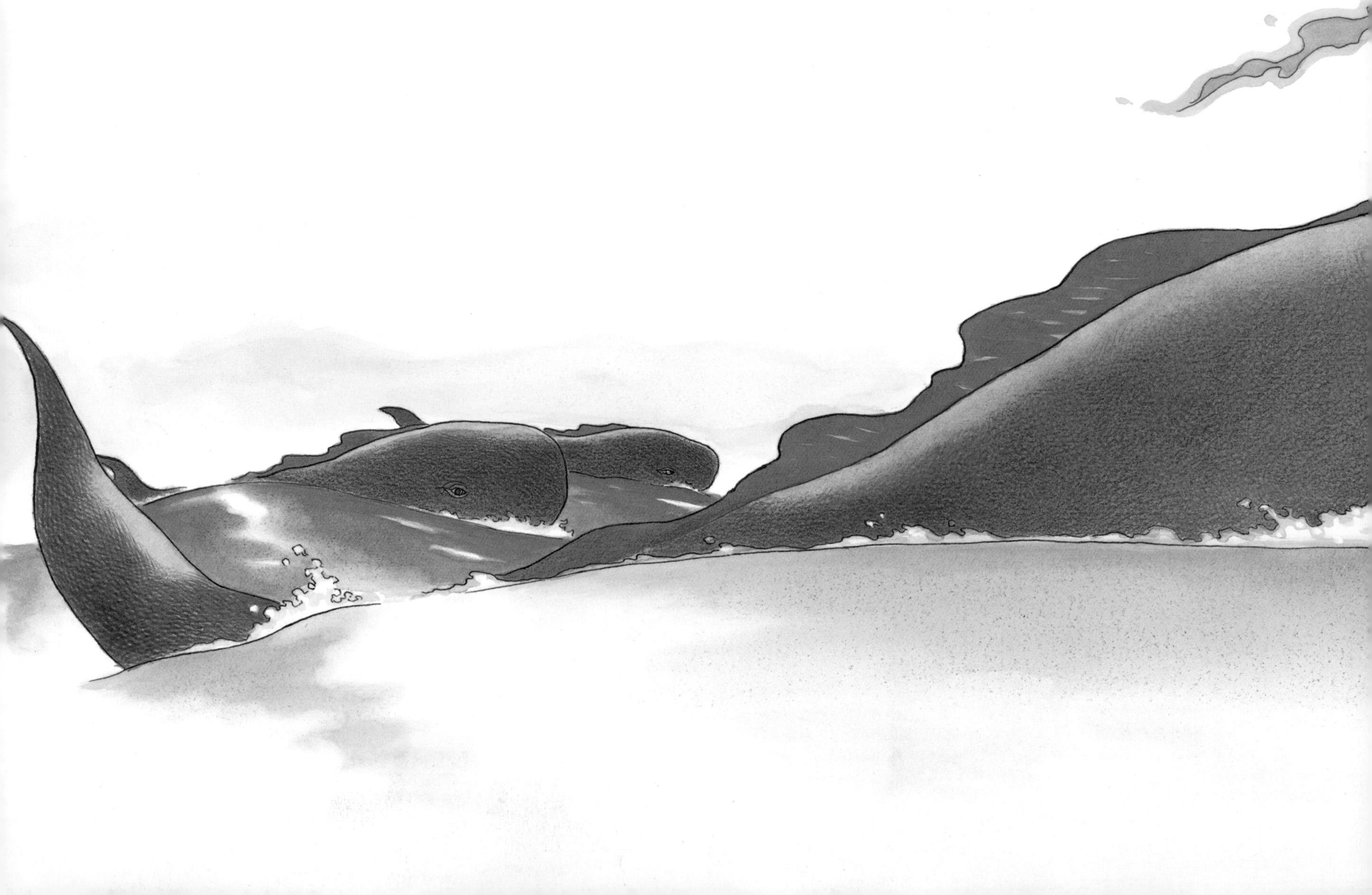

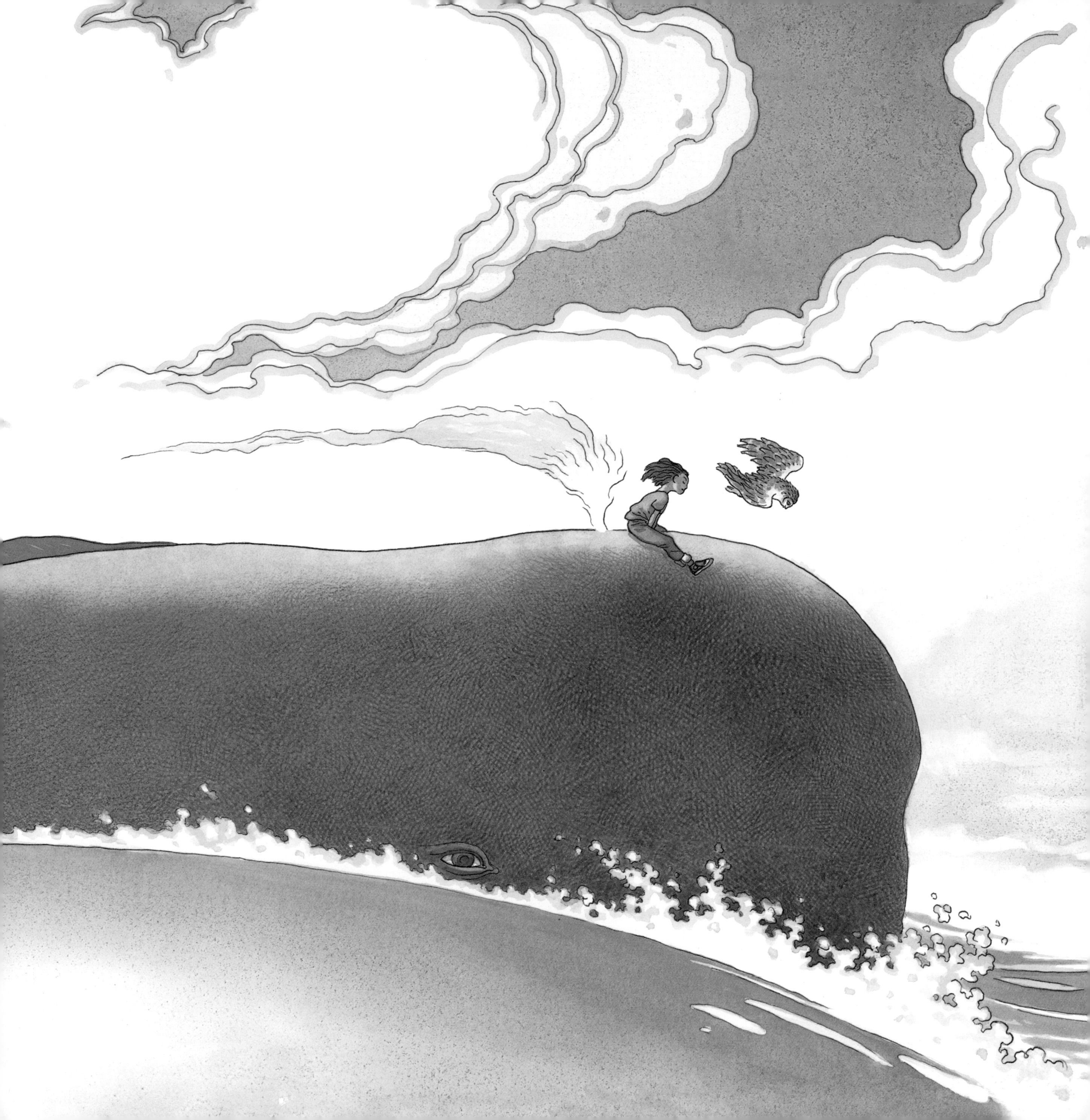

Words
can
be
worrisome,
people
complex,

motives
and
manners
unclear,

Grant her the wisdom to choose
her path right,

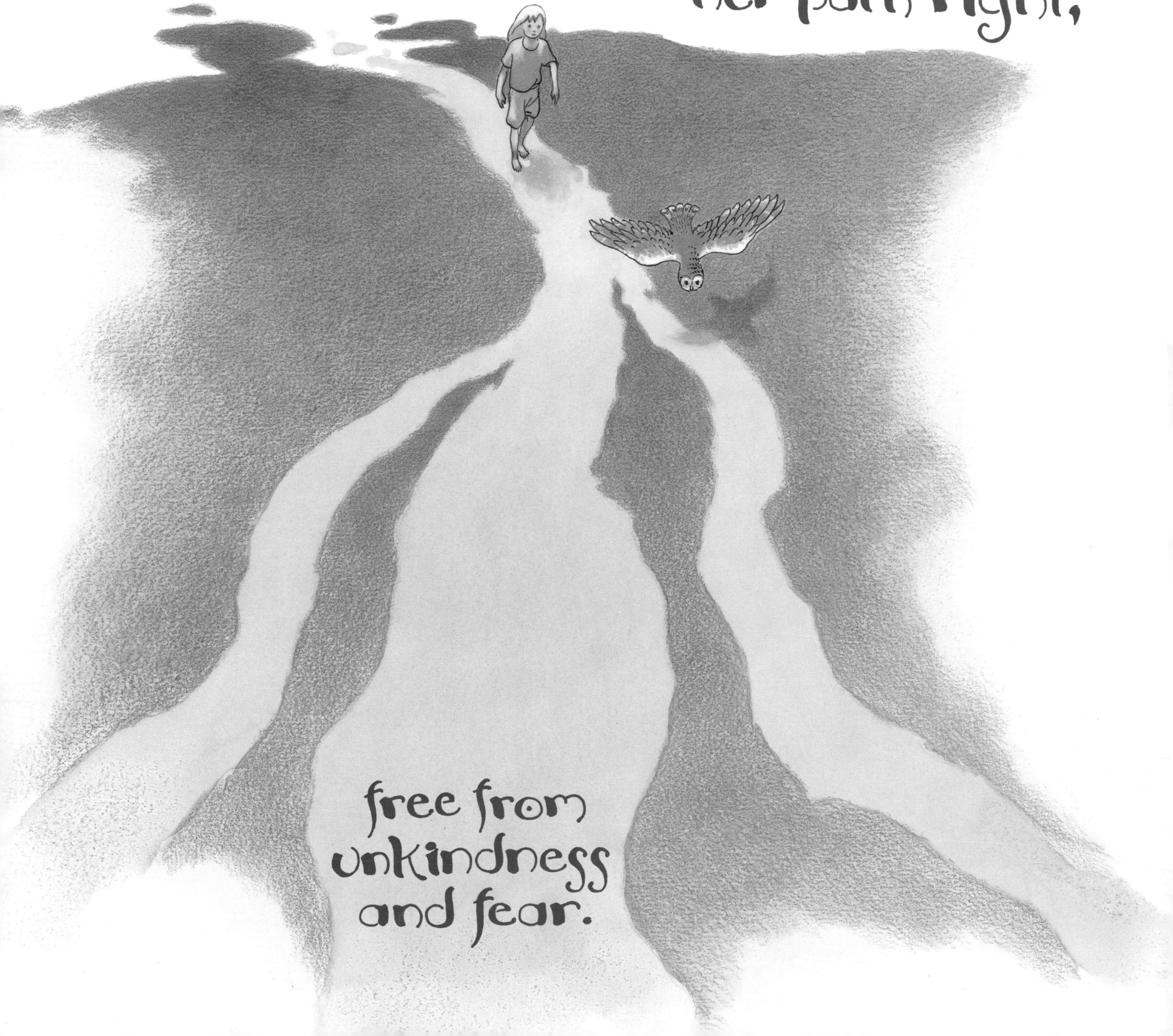

free from
unkindness
and fear.

Let her tell stories
and dance in the rain,
somersault,
tumble
and run,

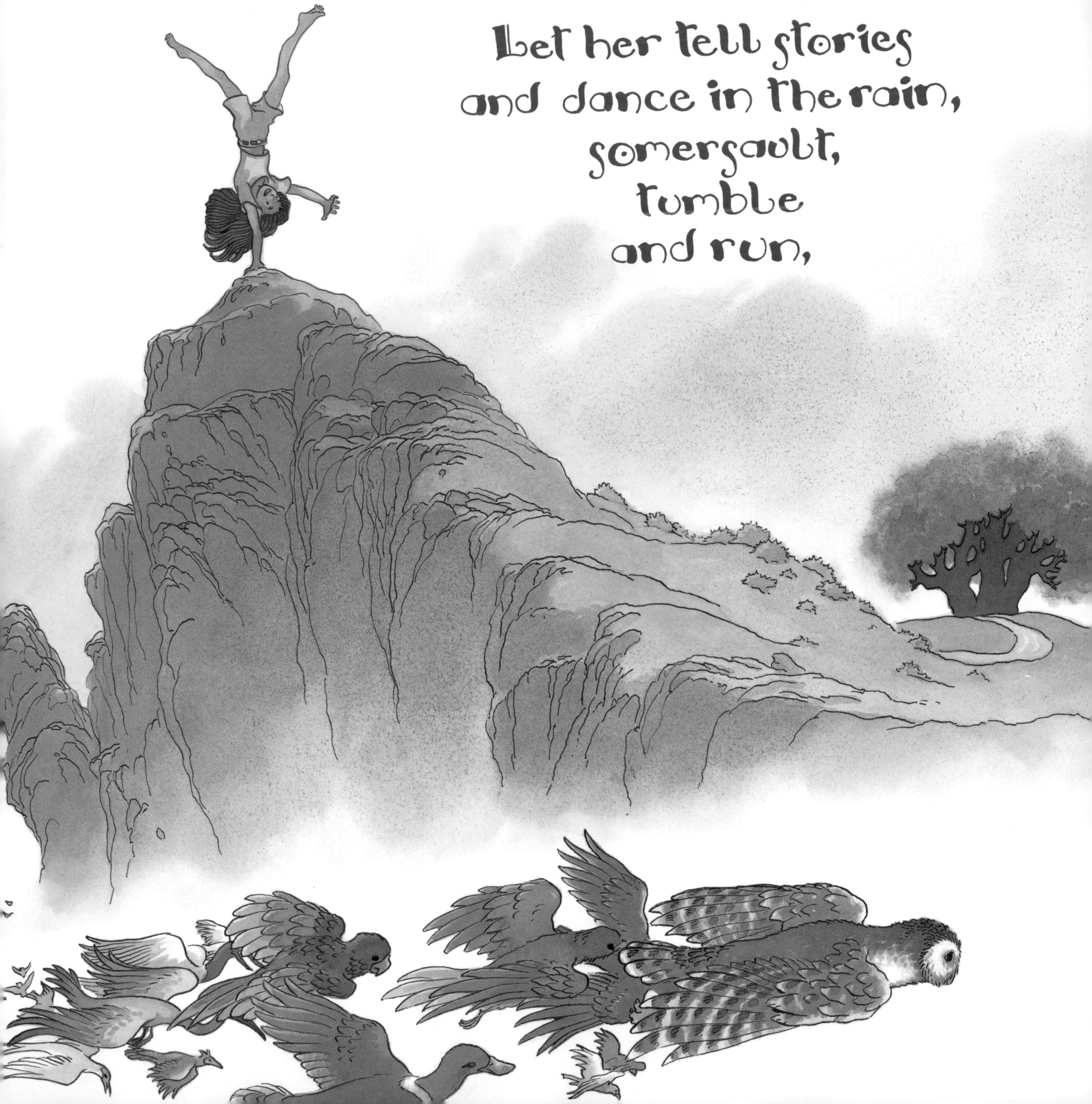

Her
joys
must
be high
as her
sorrows
are
deep.

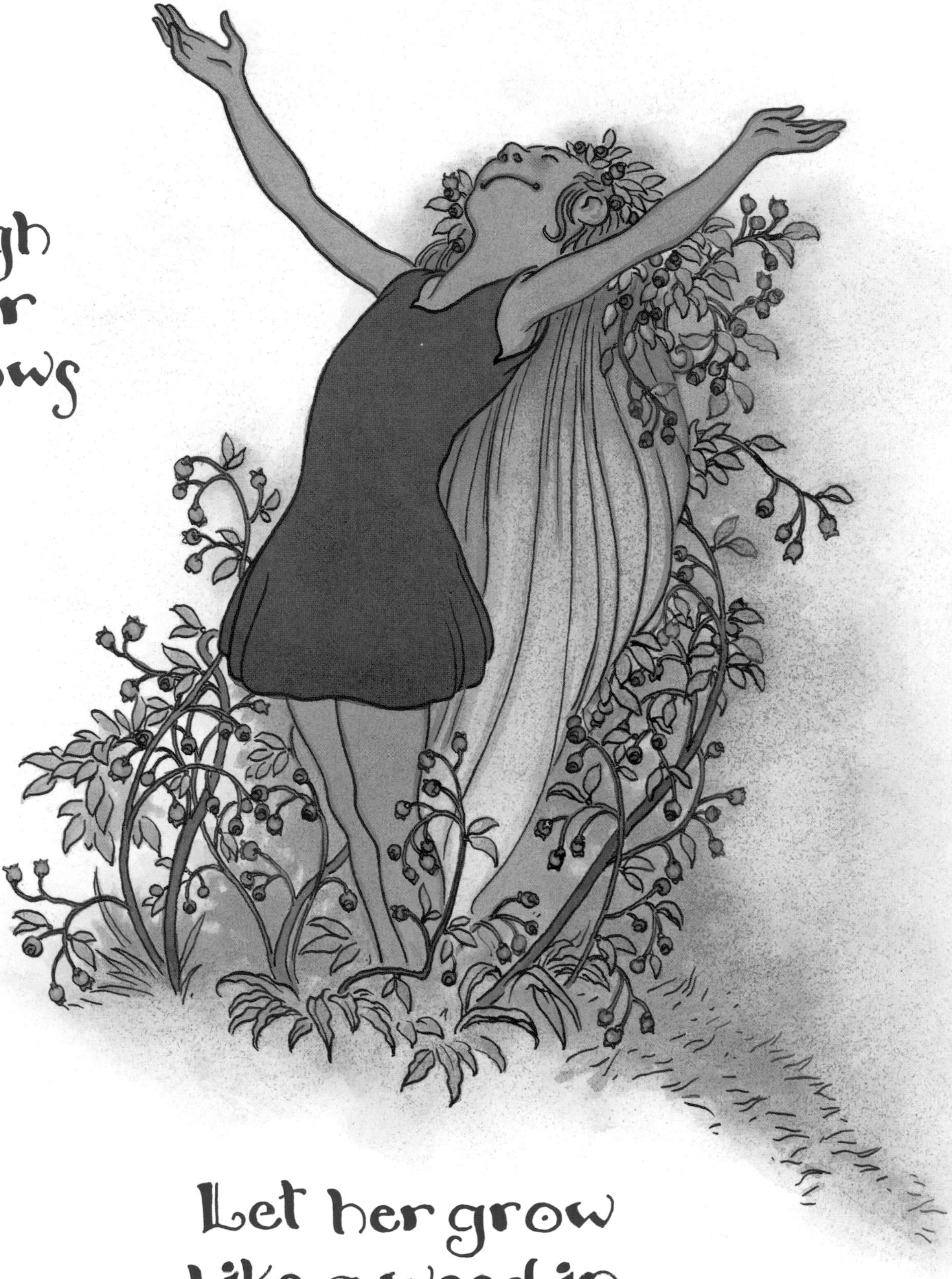

Let her grow
like a weed in
the sun.

Ladies
of
paradox,
ladies
of
measure,
ladies
of
shadows
that
fall,

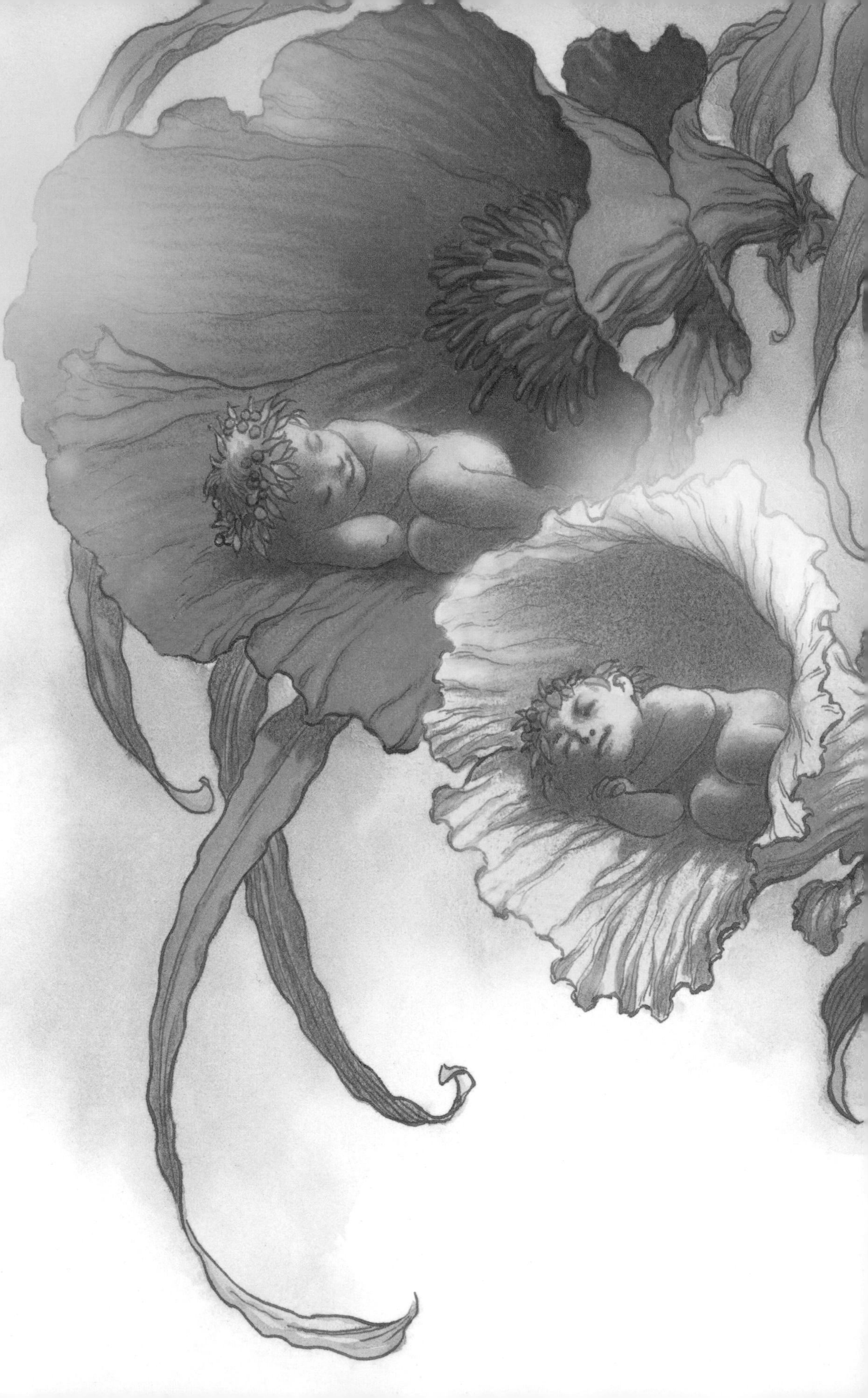

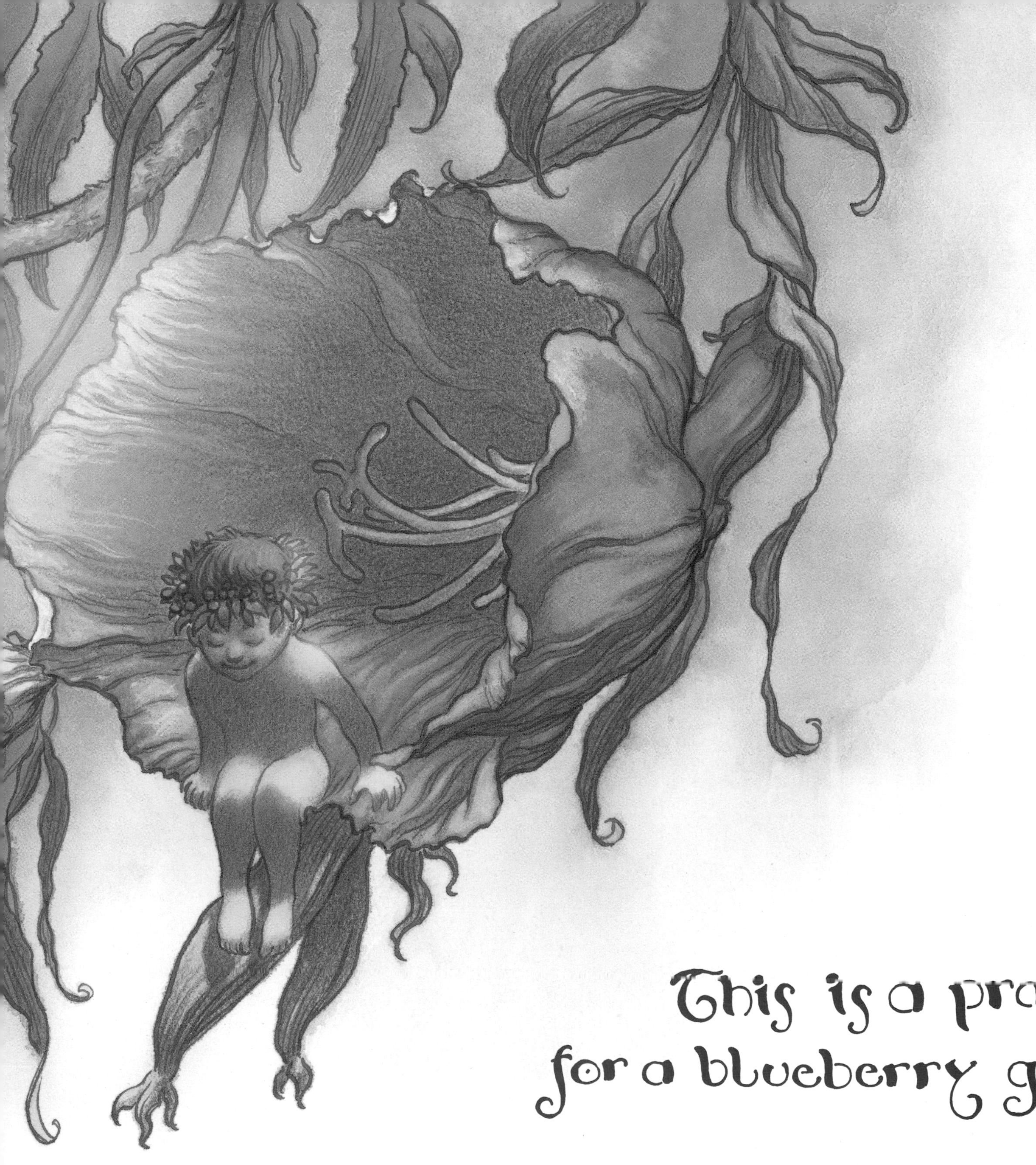

This is a prayer
for a blueberry girl.

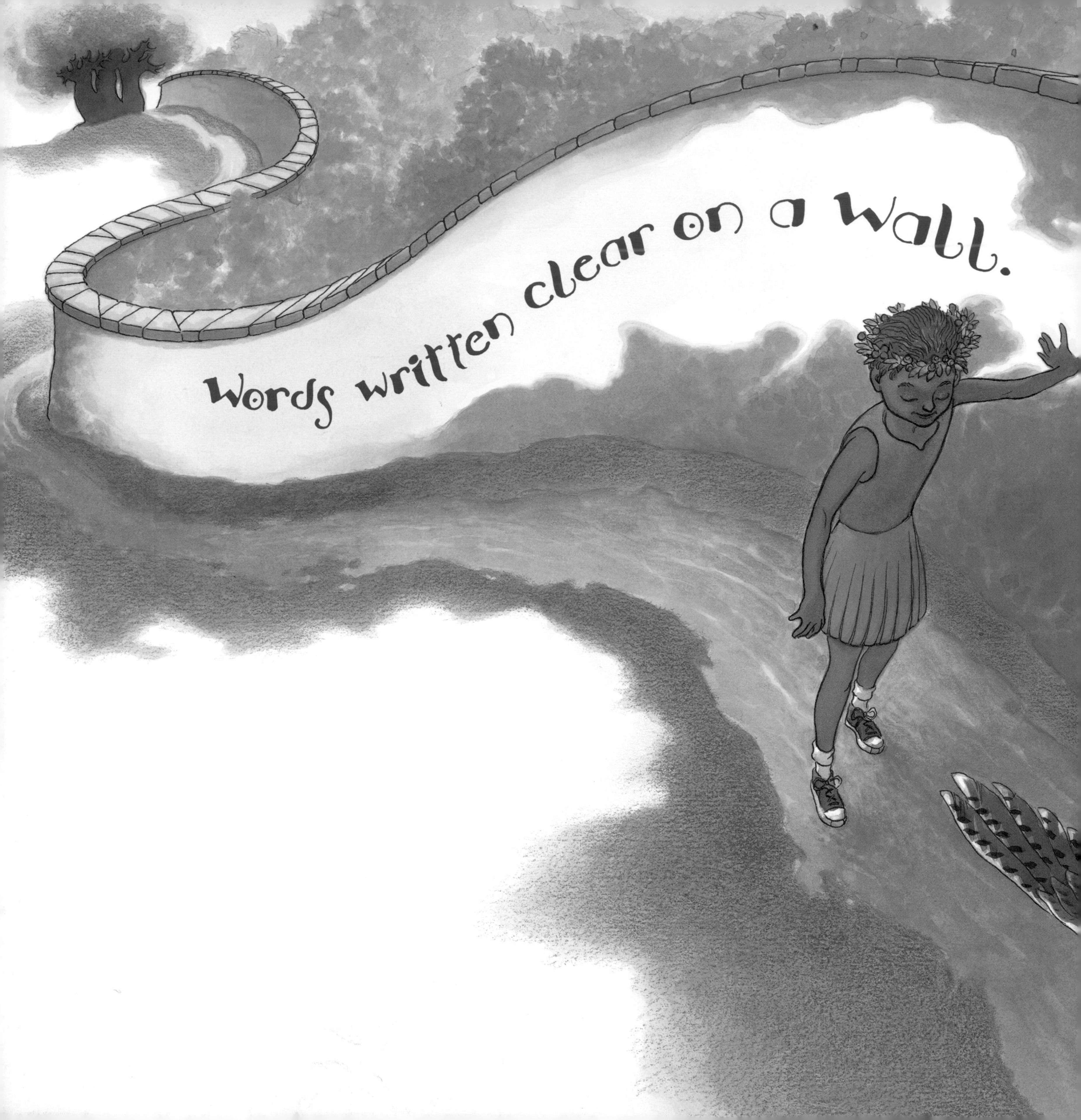

Words written clear on a wall.

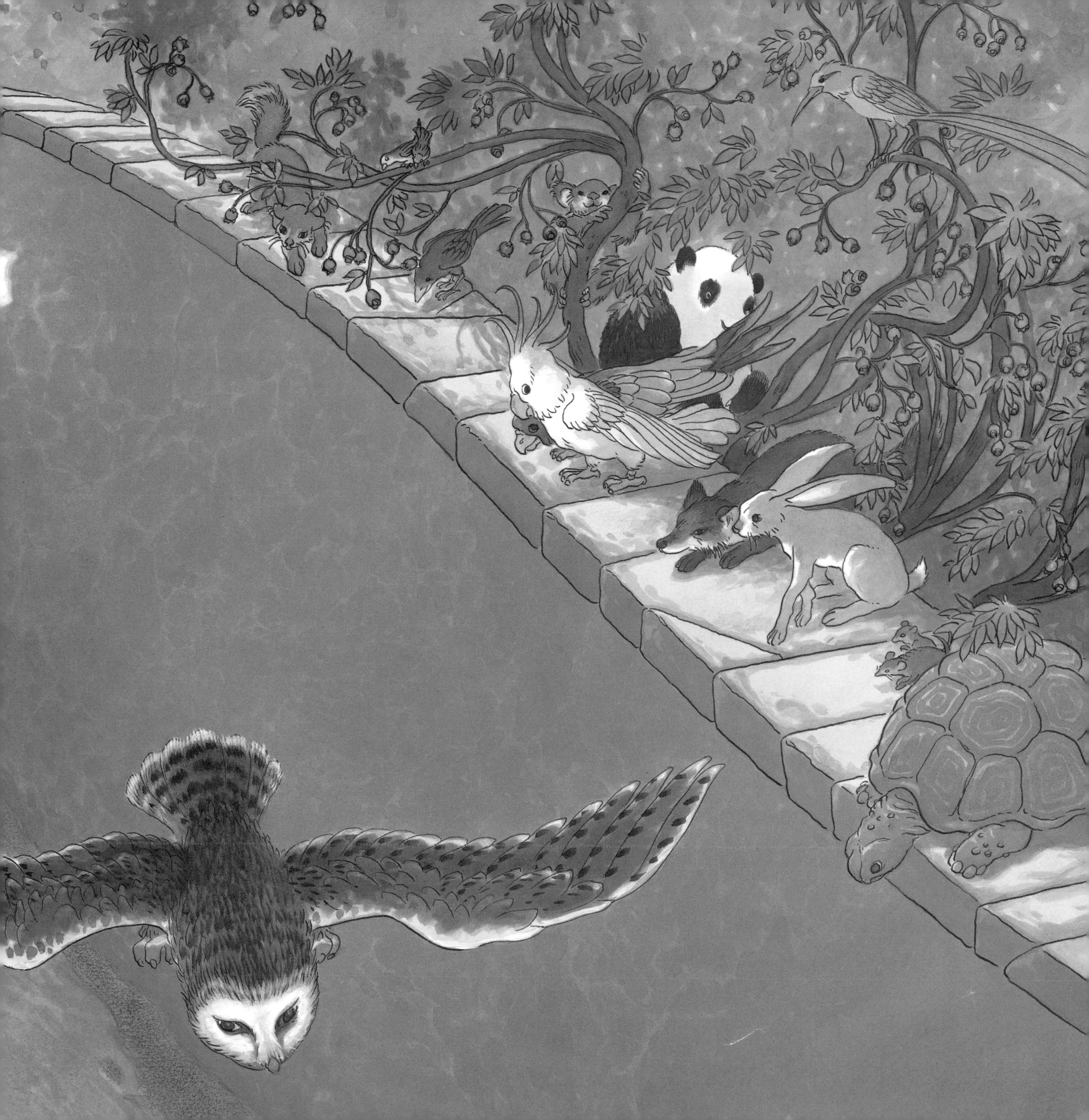

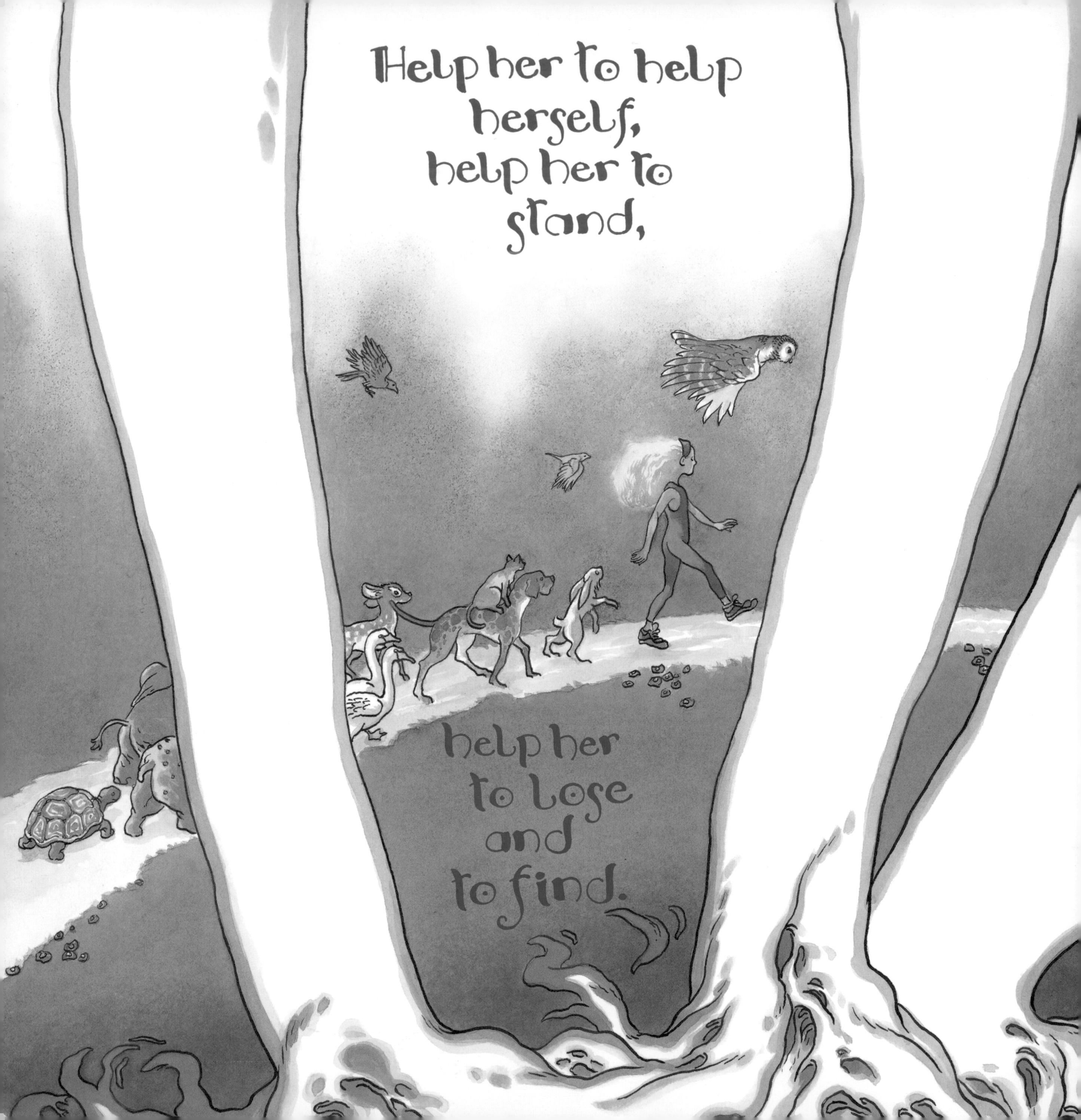

Help her to help
herself,
help her to
stand,

help her
to lose
and
to find.

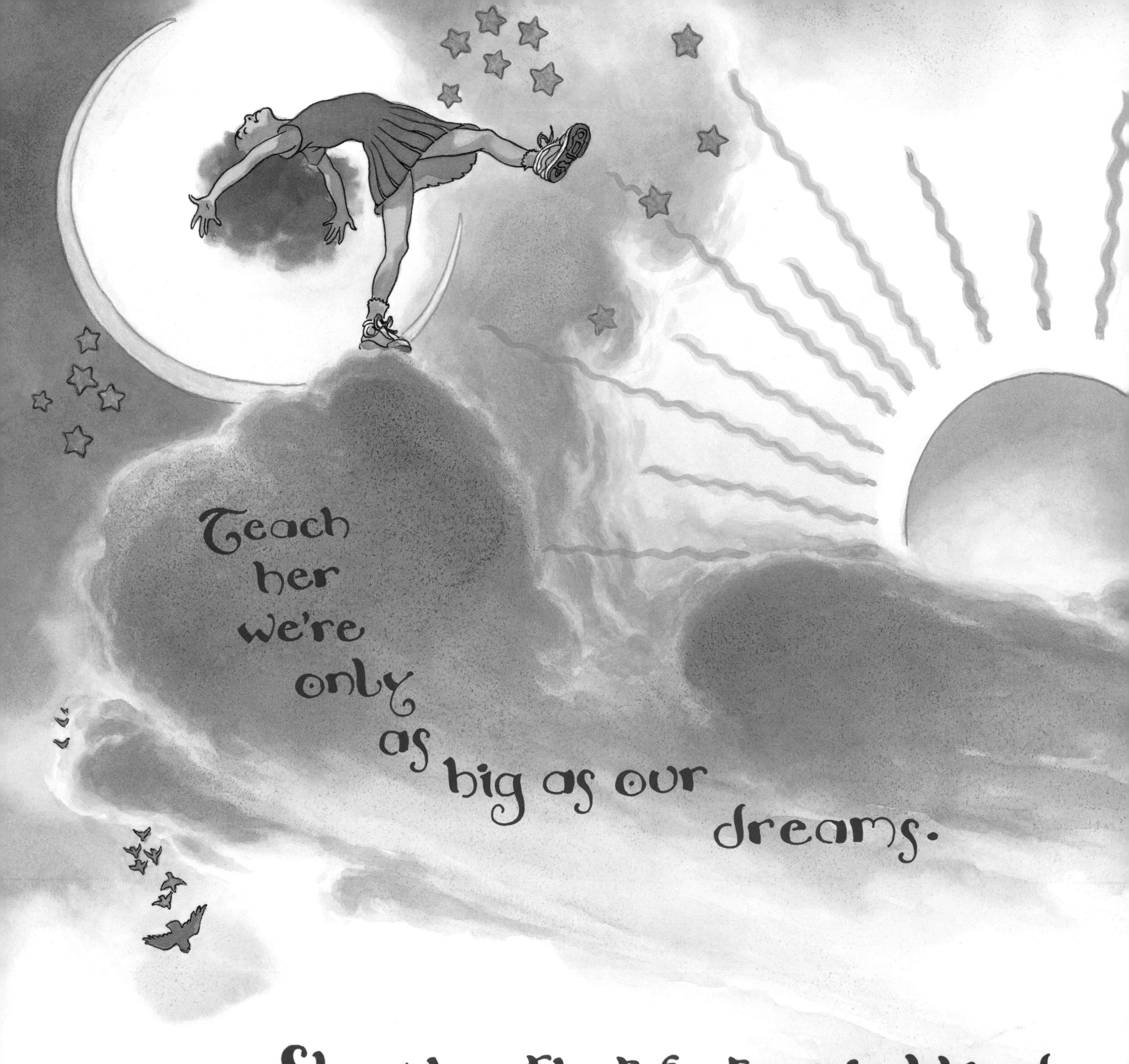

Teach her we're only as big as our dreams.

Show her that fortune is blind.

Truth is a thing she must find for herself, precious and rare as a pearl.

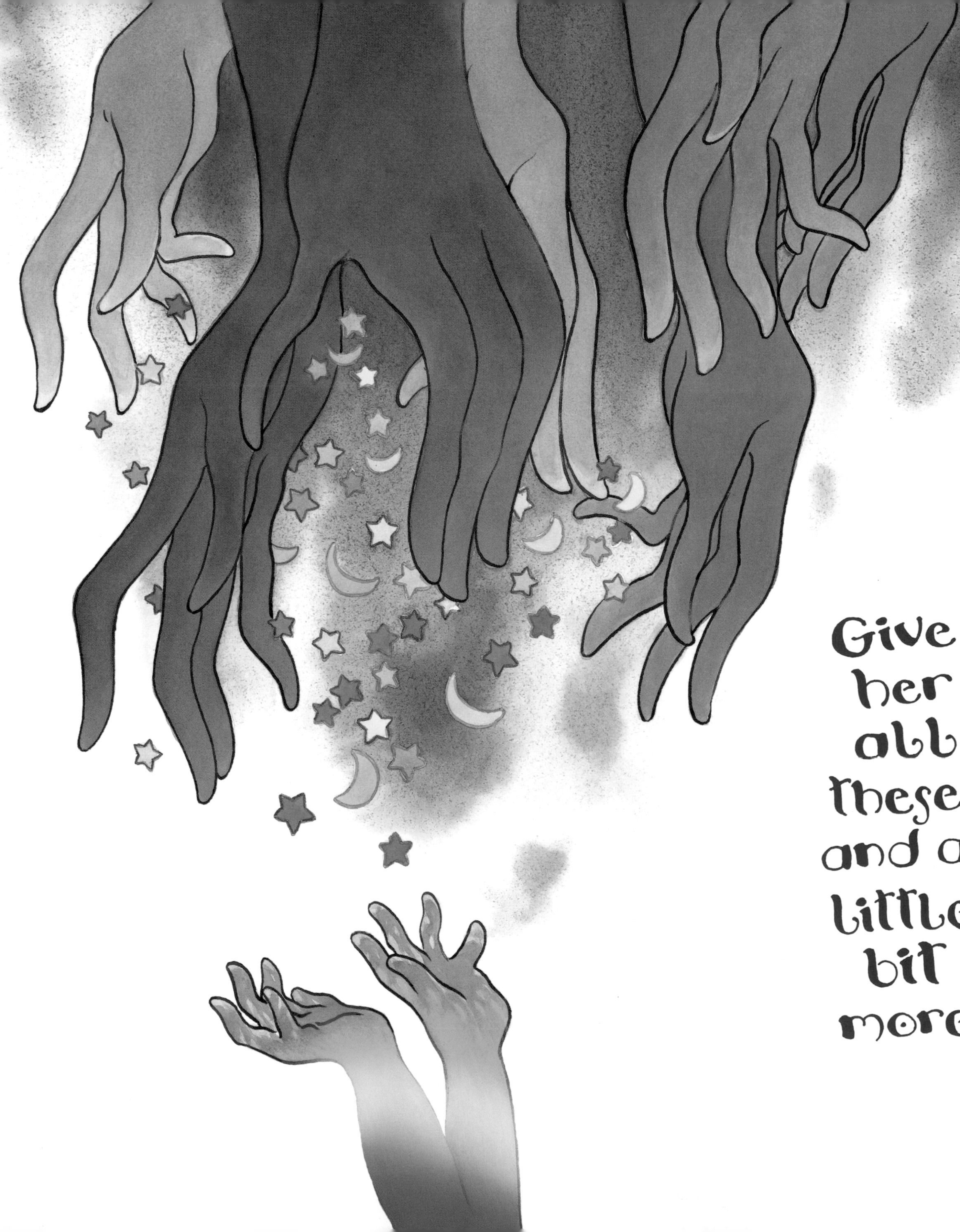

Give
her
all
these
and a
little
bit
more:

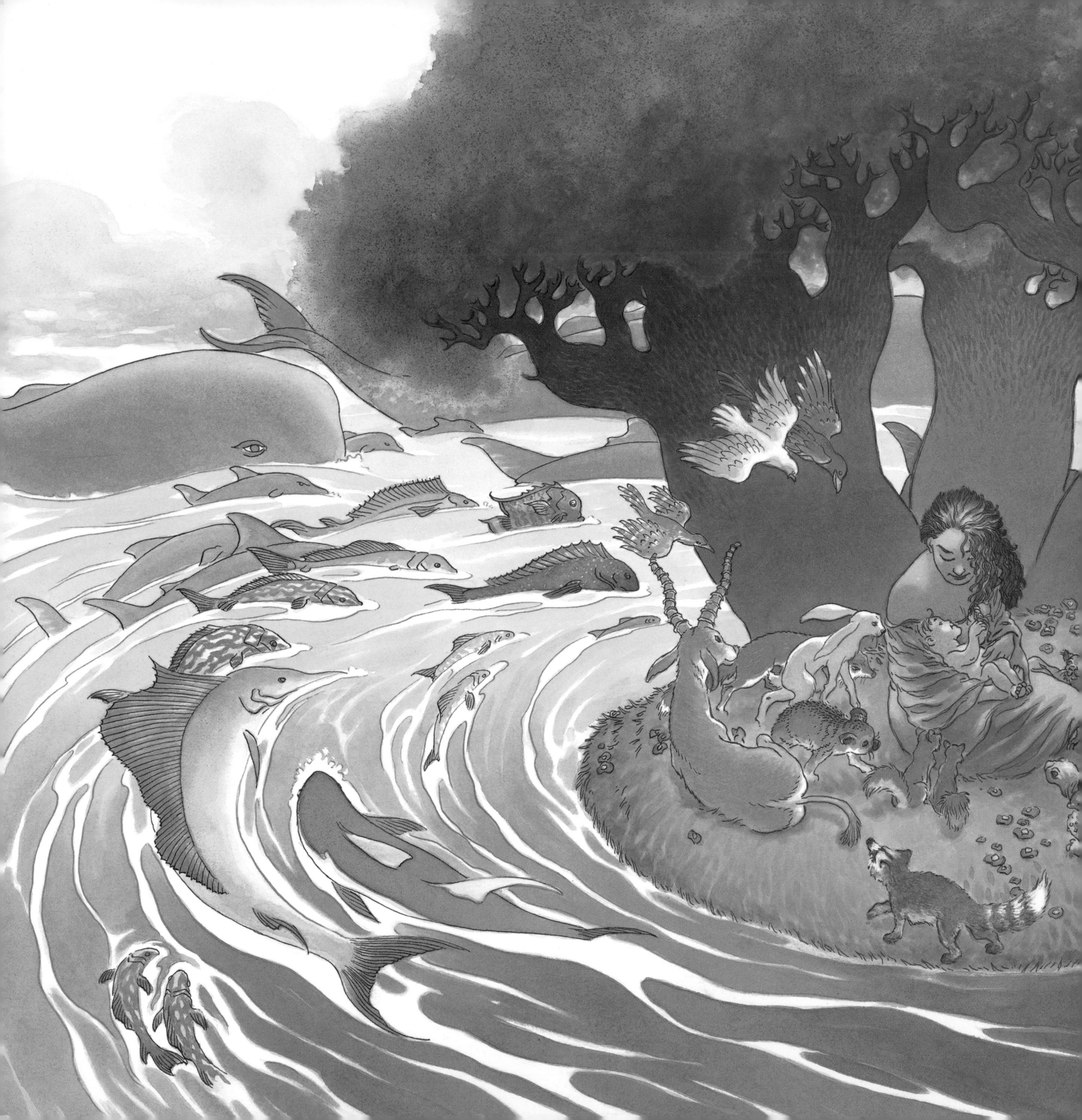

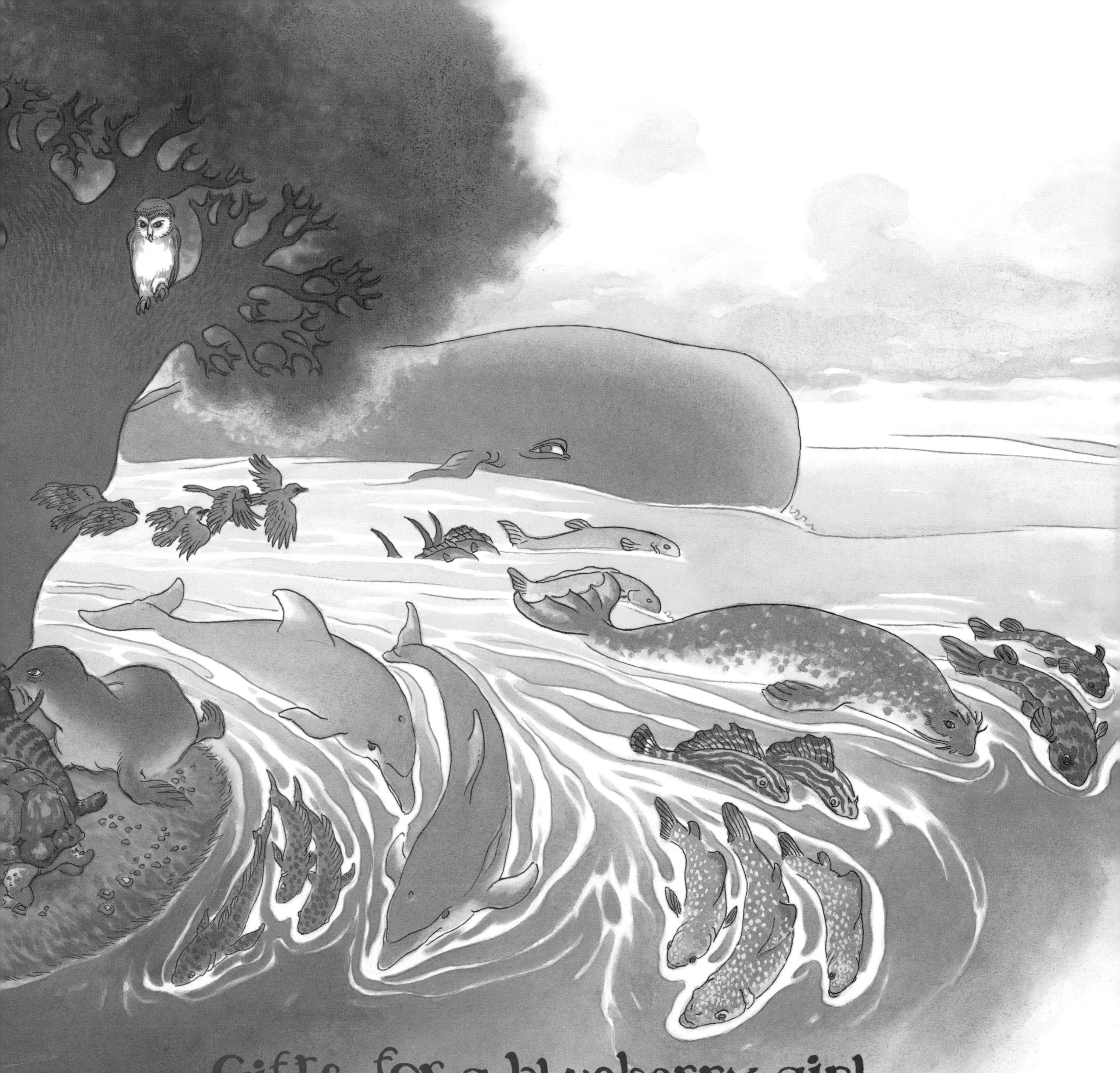

Gifts for a blueberry girl.

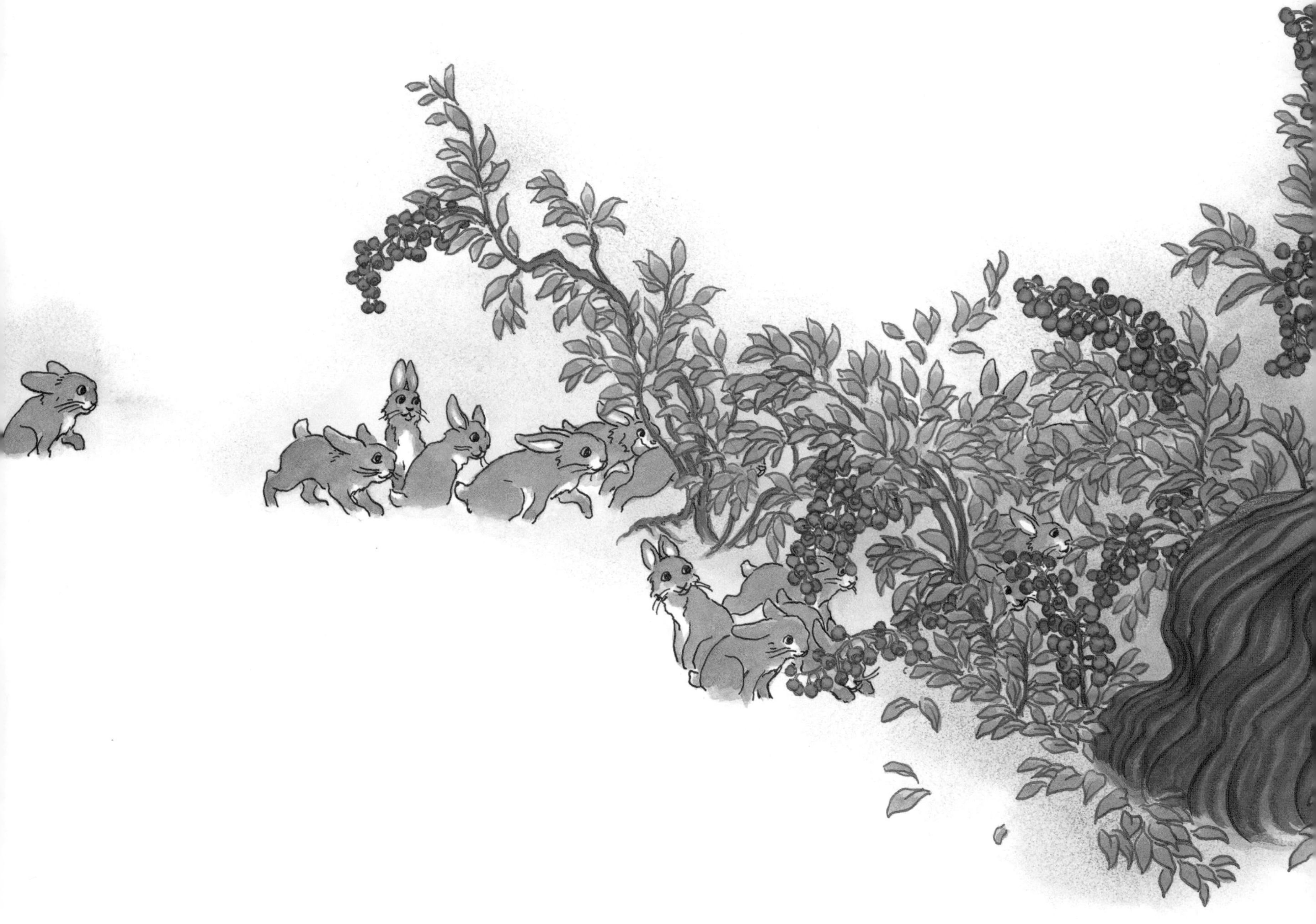

I wrote this for Tori, and for Tash, when she was only a bump and a due date. With love, Neil

This one is for my mom, who was always there for me, my first admirer and critic. All my love from your son, Charles

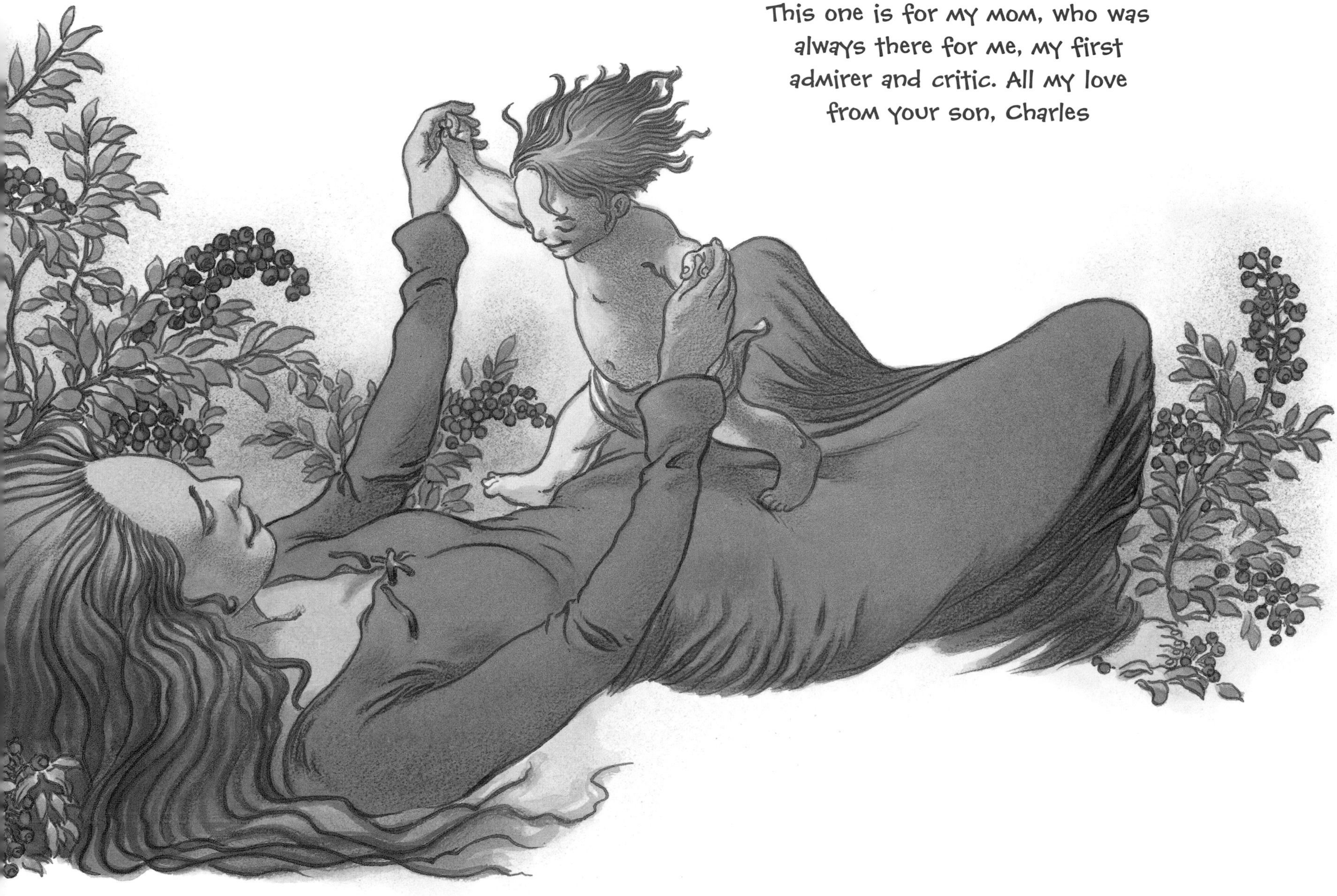

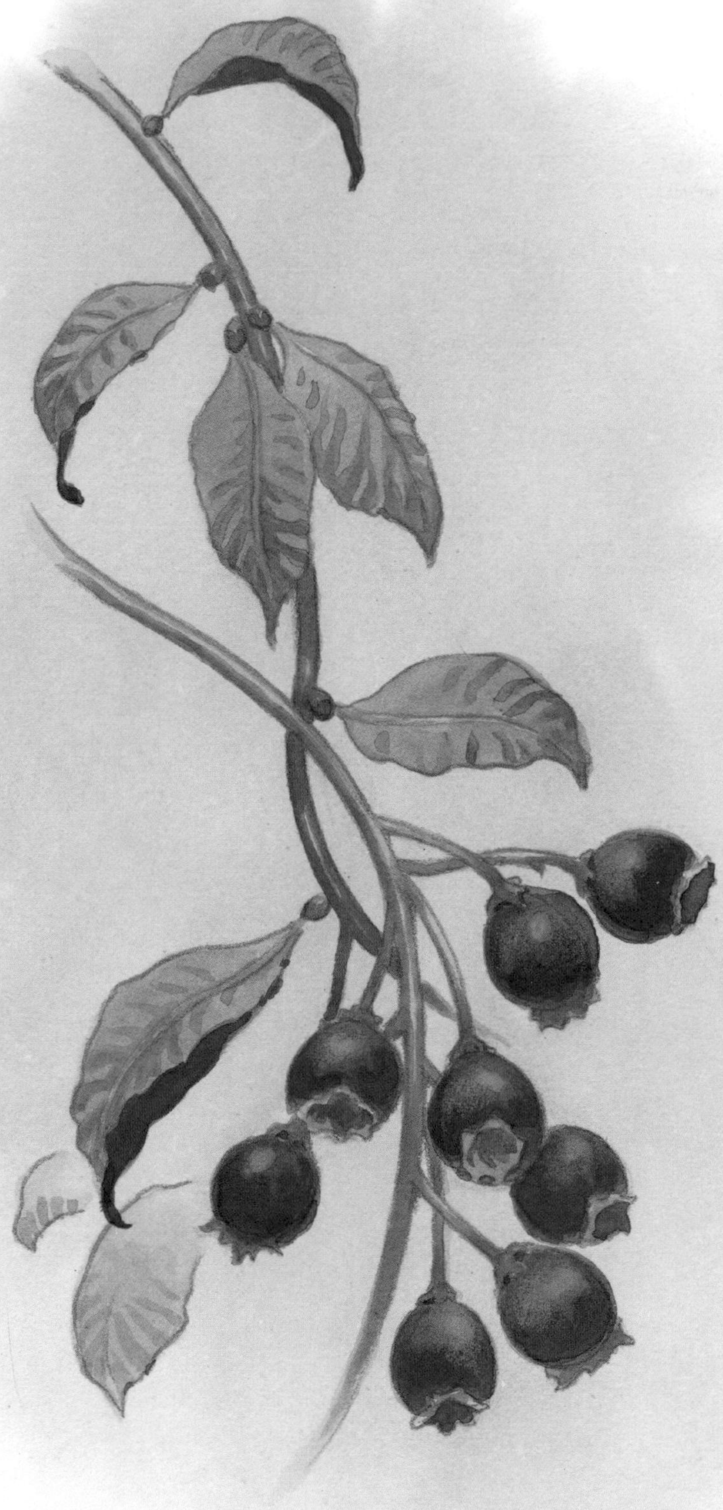

Blueberry Girl

Manufactured in China.
 For information address HarperCollins Children's Books, a division of HarperCollins Publishers, 10 East 53rd Street, New York, NY 10022.
www.harpercollinschildrens.com

Library of Congress Cataloging-in-Publication Data
Gaiman, Neil.
Blueberry girl / written by Neil Gaiman ; illustrated by Charles Vess. — 1st ed.
p. cm.
Summary: A beautiful poem of best wishes and joy for girls of all ages.
ISBN 978-0-06-083808-9 (trade bdg.)
ISBN 978-0-06-083809-6 (lib. bdg.) — ISBN 978-0-06-083810-2 (pbk.)
[1. Girls—Fiction. 2. Prayer—Fiction. 3. Stories in rhyme.]
PZ8.3.G12138
Blu 2009 2006100441
[E]—dc22 CIP
AC

Typography by Charles Vess
12 13 SCP 10
❖
First Edition